HERCULES
The Harbor Tug

by Michael O'Hearn

illustrated by Mela Lyman

ini Charlesbridge

For Lucy, Brendan, Noah, and Tyler – with oceans of love and harboring great affection.
– M.O.

For my parents, Mollie Michala and Thomas Lyman, who introduced me to the freedom of the water.
– M.L.

Published by Charlesbridge Publishing
85 Main Street, Watertown, MA 02172-4411
(617) 926-0329

Library of Congress Cataloging-in-Publication Data
O'Hearn, Michael, 1952 –
    Hercules the harbor tug / by Michael O'Hearn; illustrated by Mela Lyman.
        p.   cm.
    Summary: Noah and Tanika spend a day aboard the tugboat *Hercules*
learning about the boats and animals in the harbor.
    ISBN 0-88106-888-8 (softcover)
    [1. Boats and boating — Fiction. 2. Harbors — Fiction.] I. Lyman, Mela, ill. II. Title.
PZ7.04138He   1994
[E]—dc20   93-27191
                                                                CIP
                                                                AC

Printed in Hong Kong
10 9 8 7 6 5 4 3 2 1

Noah and Tanika were playing, when Noah's dad surprised them.

"My friend Lucy is a tugboat captain. She's asking if we want to go on the tugboat today."

Noah and Tanika jumped up, "Yes! Yes, we want to!"

When they got to the harbor, Lucy said, "Welcome aboard."

As they put on their life jackets, she said, "Our first job today is on the other side of the harbor, so let's get under way."

Lucy showed the children how she untied the lines holding the tug to the dock. They coiled the lines neatly. "Shipshape," Lucy called it.

As she started the engine, Lucy told them about the tug. "This tug was named *Hercules* just like a very strong hero in an old story. Tugboats have strong engines so they can push big ships and tow heavy barges. All those tires on the sides are there so   we don't scrape or dent the ships."

Hercules' big engine clanged out a rhythm as Lucy let Tanika and Noah take turns steering.

A ferryboat went by, carrying people and cars across the harbor.

"Why are those sea gulls following that boat?" Tanika asked Noah's dad.

"People are tossing pieces of bread into the air for the sea gulls to catch," he answered.

"Those sea gulls should be in the circus," said Tanika.

Tanika came to the wheelhouse door
and said, "Did you know that a big
sea gull is sitting on your tugboat?"

"That's Stanley," Lucy laughed.
"He acts as if this boat belongs
to him. He comes aboard the
Hercules every day and
watches what we do."

Up ahead they all saw a dredger at work. "Look," said Lucy, "it's digging mud out of the channel, where the water has to be deep enough for big ships. The dredger sucks up mud from the bottom. Long hoses carry the gunk up to a tank on the dredger's deck. It's like a giant vacuum cleaner."

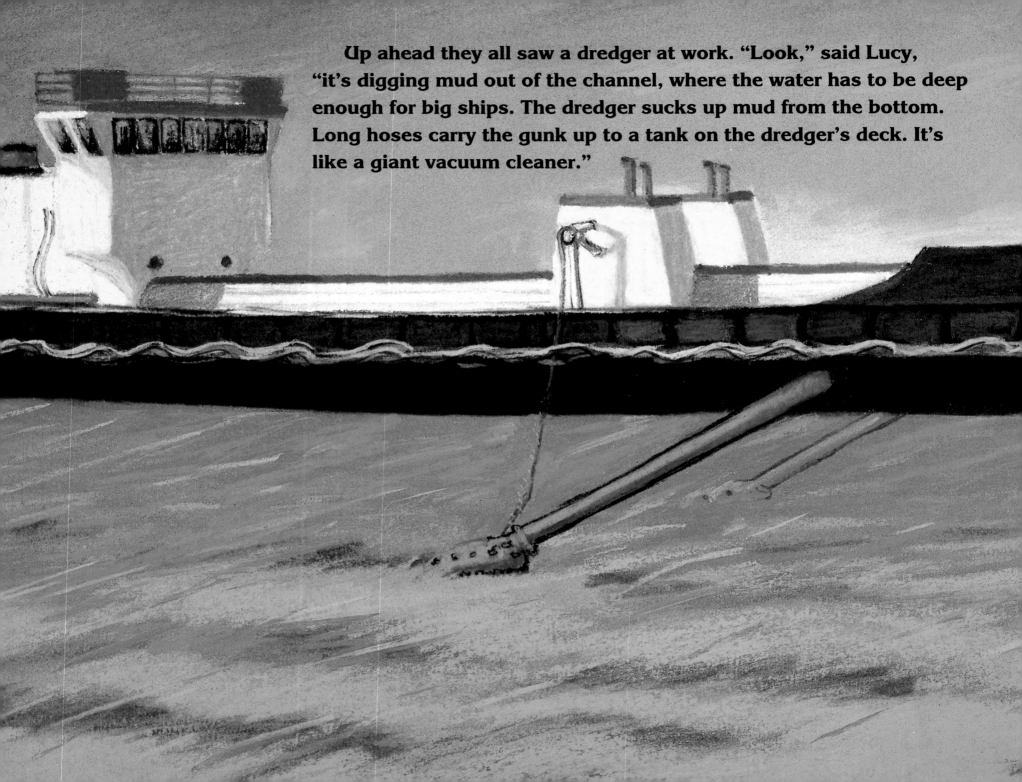

"When its tank is full, the dredger goes away from the channel and dumps its load of mud. The dredger is hinged like a door so it can open up right down the middle. Look, there's one over there opening now!"

They saw other tugboats at work as they chugged along. One big, ocean-going tug was towing an empty barge. The barge was big enough to carry a huge load of cement or crushed stone, but since a barge has no engine, it needed a tug to pull it.

As *Hercules* crossed the ship channel, Lucy said hello to the ocean-going tug by pulling a cord to toot *Hercules'* horn. It was the loudest thing Noah and Tanika had ever heard!

"May we try it?" they asked.

"Sure," Lucy said. She picked them up, one at a time, and let them blast the horn. The people on the big tug turned and waved.

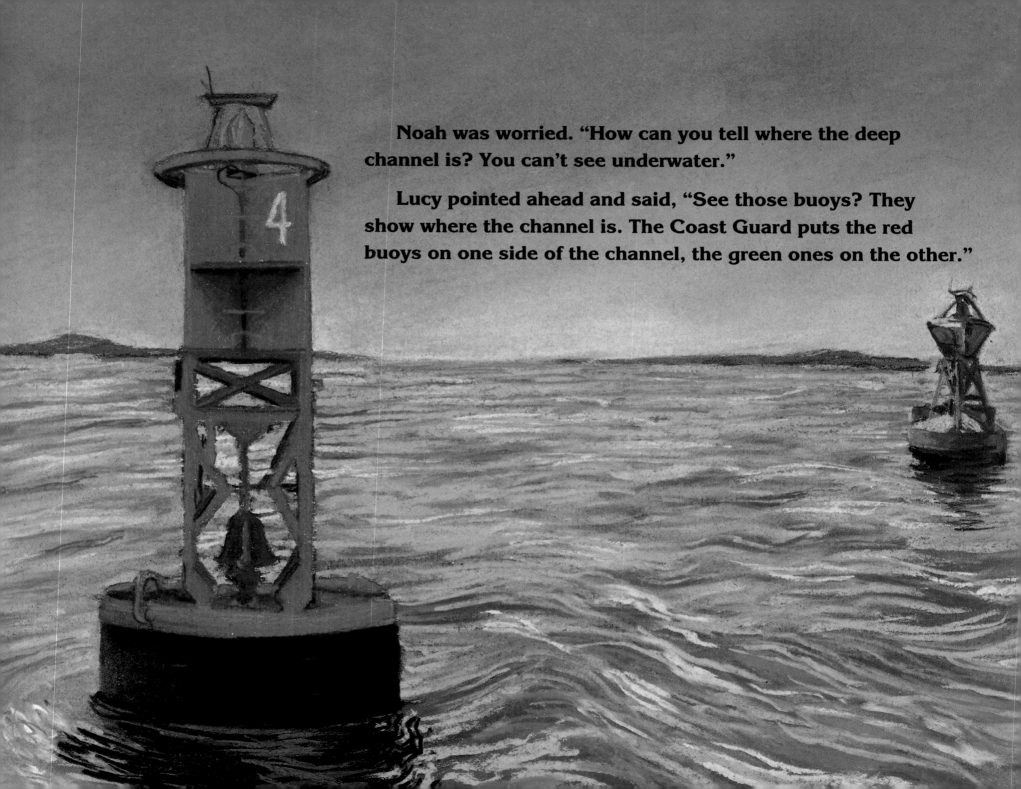

Noah was worried. "How can you tell where the deep channel is? You can't see underwater."

Lucy pointed ahead and said, "See those buoys? They show where the channel is. The Coast Guard puts the red buoys on one side of the channel, the green ones on the other."

"See this chart?" Noah's dad asked them. "It shows how deep the water is and where all the buoys are. Boat captains just have to remember this rule: *Red... Right... Returning*, which means keep the red buoys to the right side of your boat when you come into a harbor, and do the opposite when you leave the harbor."

Tanika and Noah watched as tugboats got on each side of a big ship. The tugs turned the ship and pushed it up to a pier.

Lucy said, "That ship's engines and propellers make enough power to cross the wide ocean, but in a crowded place like a harbor, the ship needs tugboats so it doesn't crash into things."

In the shipyard, they saw a huge ship being lifted out of the water. It had entered a floating dry dock that was full of water. As the water was pumped out, the dry dock floated up and lifted the ship up with it.

"Now, here's our job," said Lucy. She slowed the *Hercules* down and pointed to an old passenger boat that had sunk the night before.

"A sunken ship! Maybe there's treasure aboard!" Noah exclaimed.

"I don't know about a treasure," Lucy replied, "but it might have diesel fuel or oil on board.

If the oil leaks out it would hurt the animals in the harbor. We are going to tow an oil boom around it to keep any leaking oil in one place so it can be cleaned up."

"Are there animals in the harbor?" Tanika asked.

"Oh, yes, lots of them," Lucy told her. "There are sea gulls like Stanley, and fish, and crabs, and lobsters. You can see barnacles and mussels on the wharf pilings. And look over there — I see a seal poking his head up to see what we're doing!"

"I know something else that lives in the harbor — jellyfish!" Noah said as he looked at the water splashing by.

"Don't lean over too far," Noah's dad warned.

"You might end up swimming with them."

Lunchtime!
Lucy tied *Hercules*
to a wharf where they
could watch a crane unloading
a ship. Tanika tossed up a crust, and
Stanley, the sea gull, caught it. Soon
they were all tossing bread to Stanley.

HERCULES

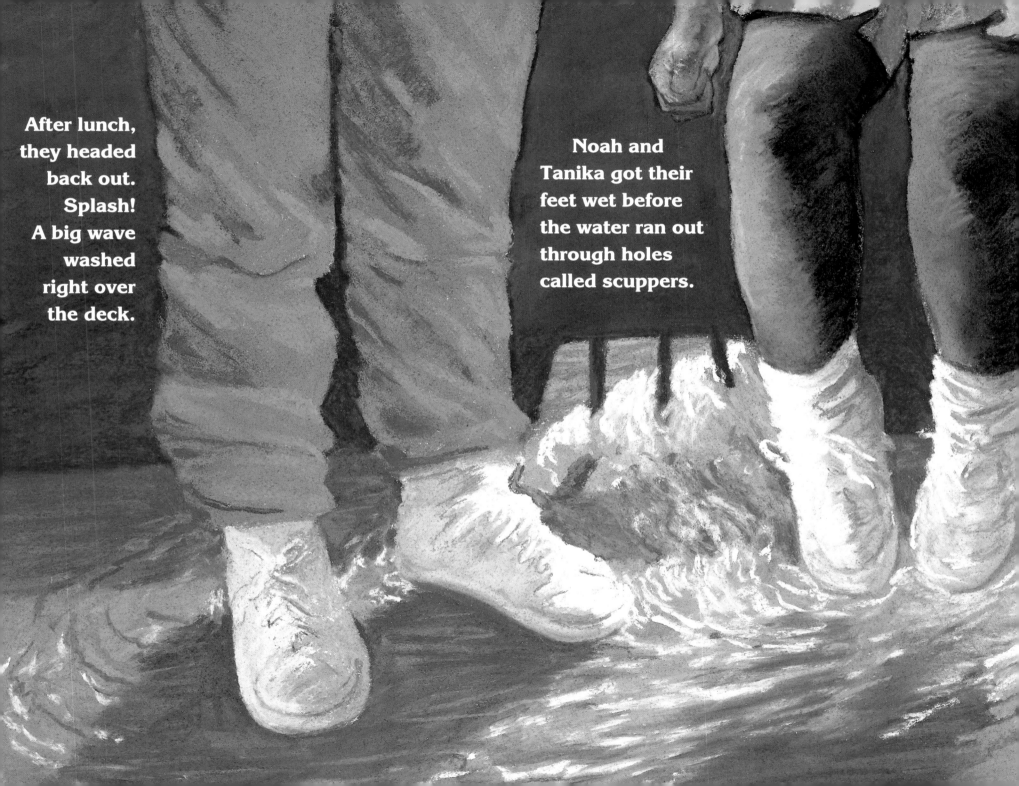

After lunch,
they headed
back out.
Splash!
A big wave
washed
right over
the deck.

Noah and
Tanika got their
feet wet before
the water ran out
through holes
called scuppers.

Their next job was to take a package of magazines and letters to a huge ship that was anchored out in the harbor, waiting for a place to dock.

"This tanker is loaded with oil from halfway around the world," Lucy said. "It's like a giant, floating barrel!"

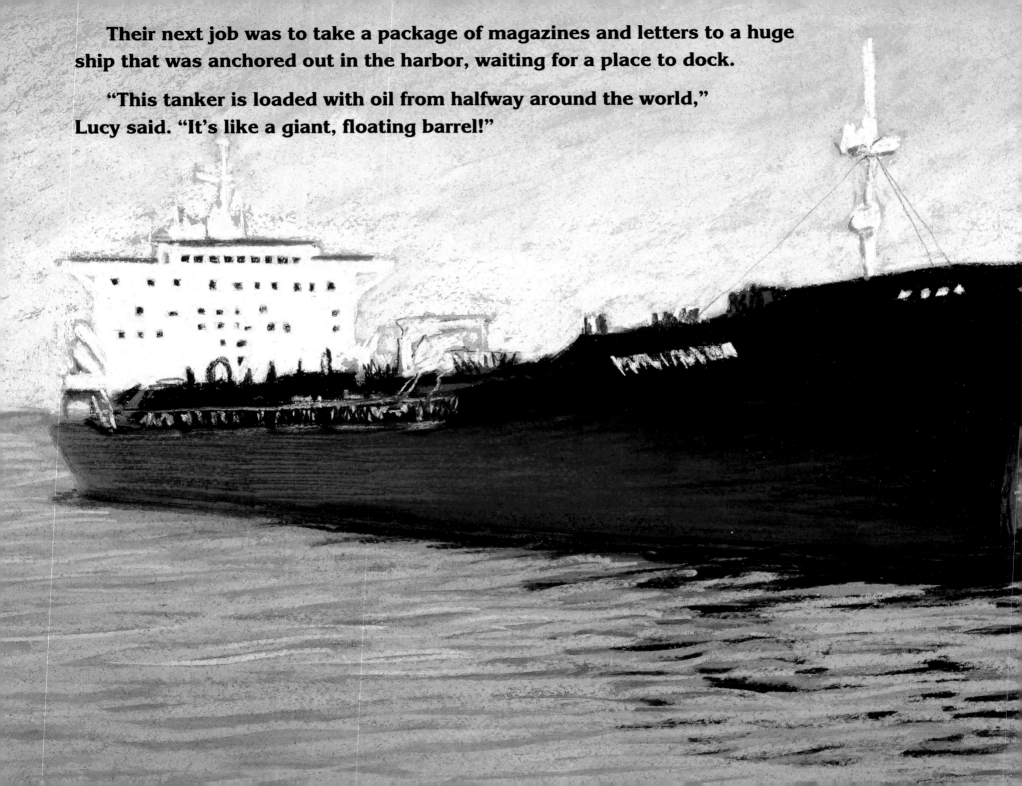

They came right up beside the tanker and saw a ladder reaching down almost to the water. The kids were invited to come on board to deliver the package of mail. The ship came from a faraway country so the sailors spoke a different language. They smiled and shook hands — people everywhere understand a smile!

Back aboard the *Hercules*, Lucy spun the wheel and headed the little, red tugboat back toward its home. On the way, they passed a lighthouse. Lucy explained, "The lighthouse warns of dangerous rocks by flashing a bright light every three seconds. Each lighthouse uses a different timing, so sailors can tell which lighthouse they see and know where they are."

Suddenly the children saw fins racing through the water ahead of the tugboat.

"Are those sharks?" Tanika asked, a little nervously.

"No, they're porpoises," Lucy told her, "and they're playing with the boat!"

After a few minutes the porpoises swam off chasing a school of fish. A trawler went by, pulling a net through the water to catch fish. Lucy steered out of its way.

Noah pointed at two long-necked birds sitting on a bell buoy. The birds dove into the water and disappeared. After a long time, they came up far away from the buoy. Noah's dad said, "Those cormorants are fishing, too."

"It seems like *everyone* has a job to do out here," Tanika said.

"What's that?" asked Noah and Tanika at the same time. They saw a boat spraying water high into the air.

"It's a fireboat," said Lucy smiling.

"What are they doing? I don't see any fire for them to put out," said Noah.

"That's what a fireboat does
when it is leading a parade,"
answered Lucy. "And I've got a
surprise for you. We are going to be
in it, too, because today is the . . . "